AF215275

ZÉLALDINUS

Also by Irwin Allan Sealy:

The China Sketchbook: A Diary (2016)
The Small Wild Goose Pagoda: An Almanac (2014)
Red: An Alphabet (2006)
The Brainfever Bird: An Illusion (2003)
The Everest Hotel: A Calendar (1998)
From Yukon to Yucatan: A Western Journey (1994)
Hero: A Fable (1991)
The Trotter-Nama: A Chronicle (1988)

ZÉLALDINUS

A MASQUE

Irwin Allan Sealy

ALEPH

in association with

almostisland

ALEPH

ALEPH BOOK COMPANY
An independent publishing firm
promoted by *Rupa Publications India*

First published in India in 2017
by Aleph Book Company
7/16 Ansari Road, Daryaganj
New Delhi 110 002

Published in association with Almost Island

Copyright © Irwin Allan Sealy 2017

The author has asserted his moral rights.

All rights reserved.

Painting on cover titled 'Parminder Sandhu (Paul)'
from the Foreign Returned series by artist Meera Sethi,
www.meerasethi.com

This is a work of fiction. Names, characters,
places and incidents are either the product of the
author's imagination or are used fictitiously and any
resemblance to any actual persons, living or dead,
events or locales is entirely coincidental.

No part of this publication may be reproduced,
transmitted, or stored in a retrieval system, in any form
or by any means, without permission in writing from
Aleph Book Company.

ISBN: 978-93-86021-07-6

1 3 5 7 9 10 8 6 4 2

Printed and bound in India by Replika Press Pvt. Ltd.

This book is sold subject to the condition that it shall
not, by way of trade or otherwise, be lent, resold, hired
out, or otherwise circulated without the publisher's
prior consent in any form of binding or cover other
than that in which it is published.

'While Zelaldinus [Jalal-ud-din Akbar, the Great Mughal] was residing at Agra, he decided to remove his court to Sikri...'

Jesuit Father Monserrate, reporting from Akbar's court to Rome, 1579

Contents

In the inner court of Akbar's palace at Fatehpur Sikri is a broad stone terrace with a chequered pattern that resembles a game board. Here, contemporary accounts say, the emperor played a kind of chess using human pieces drawn from his harem of three hundred. Costumed in various guises, schooled perhaps by a mistress of ceremonies, his women would have presented lively masques upon this stage.

Zelaldinus mounts such a pageant, glittering and fantastical, where past and present, nobles and commoners, history and fiction rub shoulders. The emperor himself, a man of limitless enthusiasms, is both chief participant and magus.

Our scene opens on the Aravalis, that chain of red hills at Sikri, played by ladies who wave lengths of billowing red muslin in the background. Enter upon the redstone stage a company of Amazons, the king's guard, who form by gymnastic evolutions a human pyramid representing the imperial capital of Fatehpur, lately built on Sikri hill. From their midst bursts a magnificent warrior, an Abyssinian eunuch resplendent in cloth-of-gold. To the booming of drums from the drum house this grandee, ordinarily the chamberlain, mounts level by level a five-tiered pavilion on whose summit waits the emperor. At the topmost step the warrior halts and bows deeply. The drumming, which has reached a crescendo, breaks off into resounding silence.

Akbar, disclosed on high, advances a half step to acknowledge the keys of the city. At that prompt the action begins on the chequered terrace, telling the story of Sikri, retelling also the story of Akbar.

Whereupon a fleet of gleaming Volvo buses appears below the palace and disgorges a Teutonic tourist army bristling with cameras.

Lastly there appears, grimed and dented, an elderly UP Roadways bus that judders to a halt outside the city wall. From it alights a single passenger, the narrator, Irv.

SUMMER

irv

i got in late at night
and took the only bed.
hotel trishul, a fright

in six colours at the foot of the red
city. pink tiled bathroom a joke
encrypted. kitchen instead

head-on, its furnace blast insinuating smoke.
no view, no starlit pillow
i slept a steep and dreamless sleep and woke

at lunchtime to a flotilla
of phulka roti scuppered by pure ghee,
mother's dal and soursweet armadillo

pumpkin. koel in the tree
disposed to prate,
phone dead, no a/c

no lady love to sate,
no desert cooler.
unfazed, koel serenades his mate,

no hint of cloud to fool her,
just prickly heat and pain
and pledges to some day bejewel her

in showers of rain.
still—Zelaldinus' city hard by, straight
up.   how could a man complain?

there we were, gate to gate
the King and i.   except that first you dree
the steep track every walker must negotiate,

pilgrim, or papal nuntio—or me.

*F*ather *Antonio Monserrate continues his letter to Rome:*

'While Zelaldinus was residing at Agra, he decided to remove his court to Sikri in accordance with the advice of a certain philosopher who was then living in a small hut on this hill.'

the saint

saint—
not philosopher.
get it right.

and *small* hut?
it's not *that* small.

anyway, whose advice?
not mine—i just
bespoke Him a son
and He took it for sooth
and went home
and did His tilth, and lo
one came along, god help us.

so He sends His missus
and the sprog, named for me
to keep me company—*me*, company!

ask any son of this soil
ask naubat singh, tiller,
what all the dhoom dhaam
was about and he'll look troubled
as if caught out in disfealty.

sons anyone can make
he means to say, abashed,
having made four

(himself not yet twenty-eight)
and three daughters.

this hill was theirs,
they ploughed and scattered in its lee,
at seedtime cursed the starlings
and the herd of bluebull
that grubbed up the green shoots.

oh, when they heard a queen was coming to live amongst them
the village was agog
and the women put on airs.

naubat ploughed and harrowed as before,
and sniffing the air for taxes
made him one son more.

Sikri Hill

Part of the Aravali range, more ancient than the Himalayas. The Aravalis shield the Gangetic plain to the east from the Great Indian Desert beneath whose sands lost rivers wander looking for the vanished ocean. For centuries red sandstone, or Agra stone, has been quarried here and travelled as far as the imperial city of Delhi.

But the redstone crown belongs to Akbar's capital, Fatehpur, the deserted citadel on Sikri hill.

the saint (before Akbar)

rock
no whale

hill

bare but
for hut

cloud
going from crocodile

no—going from long
to short

to
two

man
on red rock
shaded by cloud

all you can say

but days too i sit on a red cloud
and stupendous white millstones grind overhead

*

to tell the truth i
(desert saint, sick of speech)
came here to avoid
a plague of snails
in one wet valley

snails as big as dogs
(small dogs)

vile crunch underfoot
up every alley
in every cot
me asking have i sinned or what

*

then look what happens

i fall in love with a hill

with its dry silence
with the sound of rock splitting

the tumbling green bee eaters
twisted thorn trees

even the scorpions scuttling
you just have to be careful

the heat
well yes

*

then
november nights steal up on you
i'm given a shawl

a widow offers six almonds

*

(the sound of my voice
pleasant to me again

as shepherd *ho-o-ay*)

*

it rains here too
short rains

thundershowers that sweep by
and leave the whole hill gasping

all night the suck of countless rock mouths
under the old parched stars

*

solitude or no?

His saint

like His Majesty

is at a loss
so let me toss

this small
pierced coin.

tails!—*company*
damn

well then
one city

no more

no less

the prime minister on an eminence

already i see it spread out—His Majesty
the architect—not city but sagacity.

ship of state upon the hill, challenging the sky.
watchtower on the flat, powder magazine on high.

dovecotes endungeoned. gold hoard in some unspeci
fied keep. human chessboard on that dizzy preci

pice. tunnel to hot weather chambers fitly dank.
sewage pipes kinked, wells downhill from the water tank.

drum house competing with the elephants' trumpet
concertos. caravanserai's inhouse strumpet

obbligatos. lord high executioner thrums
instruments of beastly torture, pilliwinks, hums

a pretty tune. peacocks throng the bathhouse kiosks,
milch cattle browse upon the royal mint. neem bosks

dot the parkland, love-lies-bleeding in the lettuce.
a titter escapes the harem's marble lattice

as the deaf eunuch consorts with his skeleton
key. light turpitude invades the panopticon.

snuff godown, melon patch, string chest, camel chimney.
does *no* detail escape His Majesty's sharp eye?

omens

omens come from inside too
but the outer truly bite

the comet that hung on the horizon
a smoking javelin

a rash of cauls
a rain of frogs
cracks in walls
mange in dogs

harelips
leafshed out of season
stencil moultings in bandicoots

at twelve o'clock
on the twelfth day
of the twelfth month
at the twelfth imperial milestone
a twelve foot snakeskin
woe!

skeins of waterbirds writing the same dire alphabet over and over

and then the dreams
such tortured visitations
i was pressed shrink
to King and commoner

the King saw a date palm lead His army
a widow saw a weevil wreck her thatch
(the wonder is she told me)

should the birth of a city
occasion so much fright,
would we wall up virgins next?

so god sent nabi the fireworker
to summon comets of his own
intelligent rocketry in gold chalcedony and rose
alizarin crimson
sikri red

weal!

aphorisms of the King

- look, just go conquer sindh—I can't be everywhere at once.

- I'll dismember the man who slanders My saint with My bare hands.

- that line about redemption—run it past Me again, father whatsyourname.

- this is one country—Mine.

- you tell your king Our painters gild the sun.

- and Our singer guides the moon.

- now who's for a game of tag-the-leopard?

- My supersubtle finance minister, just close down the royal mint for a decade—simple!

- I've been thinking—if We ratchet up the pinwheel We'll lift the water twice as fast.

- You feel sorry for meateaters, lining their stomachs with souls.

- but what of Us, deaf to the artichoke's cries?

- one more thing—if all faiths are equally true, does it follow that all are equally false?

- We'll put the books here—next to the armour.

- then I'll marry her too.

- —*and* her.

- chamberlain, this pillow's soft.

Petruccioli's map

It's the best there is, and it's tucked away in an academic text. Until Attilio Petruccioli in the 1980s nobody had cared to do a proper survey. The map shows the whole length of Sikri hill— like a camel seen from above, with the citadel strung out along the spine—and the countryside round about, so you suddenly remember what everybody had forgotten, that there was a lake beyond and that that was the front of Akbar's city. Today every visitor uses the back way, by the Archaeological Survey of India's ticket gate; the ASI's writ runs here. Only the villagers of old Sikri to the north see the true face of the citadel; the townies of Fatehpur on the other side, know just the municipal end, the way the railway came. In 1900 when the Viceroy, Lord Curzon, who had long championed the restoration of Akbar's monument, prepared to bless the finished work of the ASI, a line was pushed out from Agra and a special little station built; the Vicereine would have used the Arts and Crafts tiled powder room. A little later there was a chance an English monarch would grace the little town in a ceremony of imperial succession, the British Raj replacing the Mughal, but it didn't work out. Petruccioli's map shows the elongated disposition of the stone city, imposed by nature on the original architects, and restores a sense of discarded patterns of usage, an orientation recoverable by the visitor willing to strike out into the countryside below the old Elephant Gate and walk along the old lakeshore, pressing into the cornfields that cover the old lake bed.

the ticket gate

irv takes the palace by a side door
neither tradesman nor noble
but alu puri-breakfasted bore-

geois in quo vadis sandals,
with sketchbook, no camera to declare,
only a genius for late rising. vandal

sun high, grey t-shirt clinging, slick hair,
bisleri water bottle tepid,
ten rupee ticket wilting in plein air,

the a.s.i.'s limp bromo paper so vapid
it parts along the perforation
from the counterfoil, unbuttoning the dotted

line without a sound. no peppy crepitation
no tiny luscious enfilade from childhood rites
of passage (stumbling choked with expectation

in darkened theatre dotted with dim steplights
where potato wafers perish as he grieves
because already the vampire screen fright's

begun).   instead dry scuff of dead neem leaves
on terraced sandstone flags.   and a single
dazzling sunburst off the water bottle that leaves

a gooseflesh spinal tingle
and a row of black eclipses on the retina
where fear and darkened vision mingle

in stricken patina.

the ghost

heat off flagstones crimps the air,
in silent insurrection lifts shin hair.

emaciated neem trees
in stoic discourse fan a furnace breeze.

swifts stream from the guardhouse
flicker a figure of eight mobius.

irv studies his split map side
on.   two xeroxed A4 sheets that slide

apart like twin beds
on unlucky lovers.   better heads

than his don't know if this is
jodha bai's palace (Akbar's missus)

or not.   sweat drops laze
proud on the page, transient glaze,

when suddenly he gawps—
a mirage forming not ten feet off!—jaw drops

and as the ectoplasm coalesces (as ectoplasm can)
into neither palm nor camel but preexistent man

the air fair crackles in a preternatural breeze
so squirrels freeze with upright hackles.

watermark

and then He's standing there
mild in His seersucker whites

this King of kings
light of the world
trampler of tyrants
etc
etc

Zelaldinus
Himself

watermark
of Himself

newest retracing
of the oft-copied portrait
in vincent smith
(irv's inkstained brokeback
handmedown school history hardback).

years studying Him,
always shown sideon,
poring over that king-of-diamonds profile

—scrofulous snotball schoolboy years
scoffing *howcouldtheyknowwhentherewerenocameras!*—

exact as it turns out,
down to the wattle earlobes.

i know Him right away.
He looks thirsty

on this dry hill
walled in upon a whim,
where with grim insouciance

they ran out of water.

fog seg lag

                    —*irwin!*

He recognizes me,
                    —you *here!*

and straightaway i wish i'd brought a gift,
some myrobalan comfits
or an ice candy

from the cart
He dare not approach
in the dusty town below.

                    —*but how you've changed boy!*

(so He was studying me too
out of the book.)

it's true i've changed,
hair almost gone

eye fog
jowl sag
breast lag

the old sad chaunt of middleageing
fog seg lag.

He hasn't,
one bit.

my King.

ring seal

come irv!
'E says

—just like that—
and we

fall in step
'Is Maj an' me.

do a circuit where the victory gate
beetles above the forecourt.

one ghari long He laments the state of hind,
the lassitude, the sinning, the sinned

against. what's justice, irv?
He asks. what does a man deserve?

and as we skirt the dry fountain with its chapped nozzle
i take a swig from my bisleri bottle

exchanged for one whose ring seal was in doubt
and tell him how i walked back half a mile to pour the suspect
water out

at the seller's feet. judicial reservations purse the royal lip.
rebuked, i go to offer him a sip

but turn the gesture, when i see him balk,
into the muted trumpet flourish of second swig. (He resumes
our walk.)

a man deserves, irv
He says, His mongol eye intent,

all the bitter medicine of this world to cure him of
his blithe sense of entitlement.

j'accuse

alright you made a mountain
of skulls in gujarat, Majesty, alright

you pushed aadam khan
off the agra battlements

(or had it done), alright you locked up
six deaf babes to see if nature cocked

up or intended speech. and other such
forays we'll put down to the era's mores.

but taking that courtier's wife
because she was handsome—that was

low, Highness. fair's fair,
you give her back now,

it's not too late. sin hangs in there,
it stains the air.

       He bows his tartar head and says
I'm sorry, irv, your logic stinks.

sin's a function of One's capacity to err.
in your entire life you'll risk a tenth

of what I wagered every *day*. god knows

what plays out here's not lightly done.

a monarch's slide rule clips infinity.
I wronged her, true

—and him—but let
my rights assert themselves.

great power's its own petard, its risks
absolute, its dues limitless. so stick

to your common or garden scale, boy.
this victory gate's the camel's eye,

admitting droves of such as you,
and trying only such as I.

Fatehpur (that is the 'city of victory') had been recently built by the King on his return to his seat of government after the successful termination of his Gujerat war...The citadel is two miles in circumference and embellished with towers at frequent intervals, though it has only four gates.

Father Antonio Monserrate

Buland Darwaza, the triumphal Gateway, was erected by Akbar in 1601 in commemoration of his victory over Khandesh and Ahmednagar in Southern India. Buland Darwaza is the greatest monumental structure of Akbar's entire reign. Even now it has no parallel and is the largest, loftiest and most stately in the whole of India. In its own class, it is one of the greatest in the world. The total height of the Gate above the pavement is 176 ft.

UP Tourism brochure

It is easier for a camel to pass through the eye of a needle than for a rich man to enter into the kingdom of heaven.

Matthew 19:24

The text of the inscription that surrounds the archway is from an apochryphal gospel.

saidjesussonofmarytheworldisbutabridgepassoverittotheothersideanddonotbu

victory gate

ildyourhouseuponitspendratheryourdaysinmeditationuponeternitypeacebeonhisname

the tumblers' gate

this way to the tumblers' gate, irv.
I gave the guard the slip the other night
and crept out of my own city here to meet no love,

simply to stand naked under the white
moon among the wheat stalks and jaw
with a scarecrow. my one subject who won't fright

or stoop to flattery.   you know the miniature
by basawan that shows the tumblers in their borrowed skins,
buffalo, bear, monkey, alligator?

remember the doorway bricked up as for djinns
just beyond them in the wall?   this is it.
here's where a toady ended up, HM grins.

the scarecrow got his clothes. he got a better fit
in that little space where he stands fast,
upright at last.

redstone

gum pink, not red, really   tink   tink   tink   tink   tink   tink   tink

quarried nearby   tink   tink   tink   tink   tink   tink   tink   tink

worked with saw and hammer and chisel   tink   tink   tink   tink

chisels-*zuh* plural   tink   tink   tink   tink   tink   tink   tink   tink

the finest chisel your toothpick after lunch

when the tattoo resumes   tink   tink   tink   tink   tink   tink   tink

stone tirelessly fluted gullied routed gouged   tink   tink   tink   tink

the socket filled with stone of another colour   tink   tink   tink   tink

(tan or tusk white)   tink   tink   tink   tink   tink   tink   tink

snug four hundred years   tink   tink   tink   tink   tink   tink   tink

now wobbling under the finger   here   tink   tink   tink   tink   tink

a tooth for the barbers' midden   tink   tink   tink   tink   tink   tink

tink   tink   tink   tink   tink   tink   tink   tink   tink   tink   tink

the hill a decayed mouth tink   tink   tink   tink   tink   tink   tink

history   tink   tink   tink   tink   tink   tink   tink   tink   tink

its lunch   tink   tink   tink   tink   tink   tink   tink   tink   tink

Zelaldinus is so devoted to building that he sometimes quarries stone
himself along with the other workmen.

Father Antonio Monserrate

the nine jewels

                                    —'ere boy!

HM grabs a passing tour guide
by the lug
gimme the jools.

and as the finns   and danes
freshly unvolvoed   collide

counting on his   fingers the boy begins.
M-Majesty   never mind Me.

t-tansen   the singer
d-daswanth   the painter
faizi   the poet
man singh   the warrior
todar mal   the banker
birbal   the counsellor...

six out of nine, not bad.
but next time with feeling boy.

one last twist   the taut earlobe
snaps back   and the danes move on.

At his court were nine illustrious ones, ornaments of their art, called the
Nine Jewels.

                                                    Amar Chitra Katha

the prime minister empurples

not bad for a punk, our guide! HM declares
of tiller naubat's scion —*but* this *sad specimen,*
he points to where his p.m. sits and stares

across the centuries, an inkdrop swelling on his pen
—*let's see what he has to say.* and snatching up
the page, insists i read from the persian

          'putting his foot in the stirrup of resolution
          His exalted Majesty mounts the good steed guerdon
        and tramples all who gnaw at the cob of independence.
for whence springeth our welfare if not from the thornbush of
                  submission?
      nay only under the resplendent awning of HM's grace,
          by the cheekmole of his choicest gifting,
           by the open hand of his munificence
             (and timely prostration)
                do we prosper,
    or well deserve the flatsword smack of governance
          on the buttocks of intransigence ...'

                       Abu'l Fazl, p.m.

the works

give Me the works, boy—and mind My wallop
                    (everything red sandstone unless I say)

ffirst MMajesty came the vvillage   *(duff huts)*
next the hermitage upon the hill
next the stonecutters' mosque   *(caterpillar struts)*
next the wells at the foot of the scarp
next the water wheels and aqueducts
                    (in the midst of all this an empire to build)
next the hall of judgment
next the palace called jodha bai's   *(turquoise tile roof)*
next the citadel wall
next the victory gate   *(facings buff sandstone)*
next the mosque of thanksgiving
next the throne room of the pillar
next a dreamhouse—Your Majesty's bedchamber
next a square pond with cruciform bridge
next a five-tiered pavilion   *(to catch lake breezes)*
next a school for princes
next sundry ladies' houses
next maid housing
next camel chimneys

                    (also a little garden
                    —such a garden!)

letters

towering above
literacy HM

respects the
written word.

so when
a noble

at meat
put down

his dish
too near

a scroll
His Majesty

had the
sub librarian

slippered.

How often did His Majesty turning the full measure of his attention upon a
problem solve it in a twinkling while the pen pushers were confounded!

Abu'l Fazl, p.m.

kingship

irv, I could write (if I could write) the key
definitive to this dead place, seat
of my whilom sovereignty.

this chequered court where that twit
says I played fatal chess was a pretend plain,
a grassland where I pitched my yurt

upon the steppe of my forefather tamburlane,
ancestor on my father's side. and as well
the windswept desert of changez khan, kin

on my mother's, camping in my own citadel
on nights when claustrophobia's gibbet hood
turned my dreamhouse into a living hell.

till the panicked mind, biting its own hook,
set me hopping from inlaid square to square,
now king, now queen, now knight, now saint, now rook.

the royal bath

this cruciform pool [*tour guide naubat continues to the danes*] by the royal
bedchamber or dreamhouse was the king's private bath open to the sky,
fed by water
channelled
from wells
below this
hill. On
this island
stage   reached by cause-
ways from the four sides were held evening concerts. here peerless tansen
glory of the age sang the verses of kabir, here faizi recited here music reigned.
here too on fiery afternoons in june His Majesty (on whom be peace) sat in
an underwater chamber in
air-condition
ed splendour.
let none dis
believe or
feign indiff
erence to my
inspired song.
this same pool was twice filled with copper coins for largesse of royal treasure
and (properly curtained off from plebs) pari passu a pond of royal pleasure.

statecraft

dunk the punk, irv, in his pond and look at me.
hemmed in at twenty in the fort at agra (no fence
like tutelage) twice married, twice unfree,

haunted sometimes to distraction by a sense
of my unworthiness. had I won the footrace
fair and square? did I deserve that precedence?

that gilt pommel? was it my arrow in the chase
that felled the stag—or the gamekeeper's? bent
with mistrust, sceptical, you lose face

before you've found one. when heaven sent
a boar's tusk frees you. the body politic
(me) gashed thigh to thigh out hunting. rent,

spatchcocked, put out to grass, not really sick,
you stray into building. limestone, mortar,
brick and stone, shovel and pick,

neglected sages, unveil their fair daughter,
design. I start with miriam.
fresco blond seraphs in her bedding quarter

so my luso-christian wife feels at home,
and look where I end up—founding a faith
of faiths whose temple is my throne room.

destiny? auto-da-fe?
consider my famed syncretic pillar.   axis
of state, bred from loins that tempted fate

(near miss that tusk).   faith or praxis?
hinduchristianturk prop up my diwan-i-khas,
so you could say at their imperilled nexus

the legs of state stand firm. just a trace,
the scar now, irv—see?—but how the old hurts persist,
seething in men and nations under the cicatrice!

the throne room

so leave young naubat to his might-
have-beens, irv (poor boy, what a job!)
and mark that stone totem, my stalagmite

of state (a guide takes many knocks. did I fob
him off ungently? should I have given
him a purse? six villages? made him nabob?)

lynchpin of the throne room, my carven
column of ecumene.   watch that pale dane
lean on it as he makes a dolmen

wish. mousewhite lashes blinking as both hands strain
to meet and clasp behind his corrugated back.
that's me, irv. not all chain

mail of conquest. that's my peacetime rack.
you know how it is, irv, you
turn god's own aroused amnesiac—

you have to fangle something new!
but no, they want the foreign style of shoe.
our best wits emigrate to truckle and kowtow,

kiss new york ass (oh, they'll say kick)
brown nose in london, walk that talk (curl toes
passé). fact is, irwin, they're stuck

there in bad faith, ventriloquizing as
the centre shifts away from rome—migrates back
home. who'll break the bad news to our outsauce boys?

your deepest dreaming's *here*! wake
up, put your body where your mouth is.
slip on agra shoeleather. talk

from here! look, irv, every faith's
graven on this menhir, see?
sometimes I think—that's no axis

of the universe—that's Me*!*

(maybe I'll give the punk bihar?)

imperial farman   [frayed]

                              He is rich
the Great the Great
                              [seal]
                                              commands that
                         naubat singh tour guide

      great great great [x 12] grandson of naubat singh, tiller

      himself great great [x6] grandson of naubat singh, tanner

         [?] [acres?] [paces?] of prime agri[cultural land?]

            [in?] [adjoining?]   the province of b[i]har

Whereupon, whereby, wherefore, and whereunto it is incumbent
on him to

pay estate [?] tax and

                       tax and

        [moreover?]   escheat duty

                              a[nd] to append there[with?] an

easement

                                              nowise

this day the 12th of [Never?] [Nove*mb*er?]   henceunto
                                       [—hence*unto*??]

princeling

the sunken garden, irv.   see that boy
by the gazebo there?   watch him pace
the lawn reciting as he walks, no childish toy

to distract him, oblivious of the water race
whose stonecut fish-scale motif
ruffles crystal water into lace.

my grandson.   who, when he can relieve
my toper son, will rule (he'll build the taj mahal)
transmuting low to high relief.

nine years old!   no better age in all
the world.   at his age I was storm-tossed
dragged through mountain passes in my father's thrall,

fugitive in Afghanistan, his kingdom lost
(my schooling too).   I learnt to count with rukhs
I learnt to skip and run with cheetahs, crossed

icy streams, burning desert sands, made fishhooks
of nibs.   an intellectual's son who cannot hold a pen.
why to this day I love the smell of books

and fumigate my schoolmen.

schoolmen

some day I'll show you, irv, he says to me,
the schoolmen at their labours
(leading me past the princeling's academy),

grown men writing term papers,
magicians turning books
into books. Myself, I'd sooner fence with tapers.

over there you see the social cooks,
hunger theorists basting their fatted calf.
this handspun lot are nativists. that inglenook's

a den for those who labour on behalf
— jobbing activists, thespians of rage.
here salaried professors rig a graph.

this one I pay a handsome daily wage
for laundering used paper. watch nature
cure spent learning page by page.

now this sage here, complete with cranial suture,
they say he has a glass prospective
of wondrous power for winkling out the future,

but hearing, when refuted, conveniently defective.
I took his mealy mouth out to dine at timur
and watched him squirm (it gives perspective).

the décor, menu, chintz, the pinchbeck glamour,
small town crappyola, narrowly appraise
our friend's big appyola distressed amour

propre. fuck this charade, irv, let's go gormandize.
smells like the kitchen's done its friday vegan lamb
swamped in horseradish sauce. do catechize

your neighbour doctor nurture (watch him cram)
tell him our higher learning stinks
because our hungriest are on the lam

in boston town, and while they sing
songs of exile, indologize, and praise
our growing g.d.p, sikri's e.q. shrinks,

and tabulators mock our sad malaise.
exile—my *dick*! what keeps them there?
it makes me sick. their winning ways?

level sidewalks? a cutprice return fare?
that global-village mantra? 4G wifi?
trading circumference for centre (*there*

of course) for what? to live with the jaundiced eye?
where the best you can hope for is villain
to indiana jones, where massa has you by

the short and curlies? that's craven, irv, craven!
even by our fallen standards, that's debased.
is the job worth it? *is* it irwin!

all right so cowdusk's not to everybody's taste
—truth is it's always been outsiders
not bespoke natives, cranially chaste,

who made us see what's right beside us,
see through this defaulting citizenry.
stout foulweather friends, max muller, mohandas,

and such. their scholars *still* do the lion's share
of serious work—their kramriches and koches
but *our* export experts? what keeps them there?

the loot? the armani suit? the porsches?
jesus, irv (peace upon his name, but by his rood)
I'd sooner wear rags, clip my moustaches,

cut my throat—read my dewlap! god knows I could
endure that costly gutter-crawling, but then they speak
for us as if they lived here, shared the common good

and bad. look. I say, go there. great. go seek
your fortune.   become that. be
that. write that glowing moment. speak

your new land, its manifest destiny.
write that thing. set yourself free!
that's how it should be with immigrants, pakistani

greek, scots, armenian—belong! put on that me.
why fly this sorry flag? I mean we mughal crew
shook off that turki dust, dug in and ploughed *this* lea.

what keeps them there? damned if I know.
this one goes from chat show to chautauqua to chair,
that one foists on all who care his tortured photo.

not one of them (well, maybe one) has paid his way—
that fatwa fellow. the rest doing a hitch hike
on the gravy train (injun end) while beavering away

at their bleeding c.v. for holy miriam's sake,
what keeps them there! the footlight basking?
the thrill of being closer to the mike?

—but what, forgive me, irv, for asking
(this politely, not meaning to chase
and corner) do *you* do when you're tasking?

i blench and stammer in the face
of his harangue. —*i—i write
Highness*. and He, unlettered, lets that cook a space,

then turns and skewers my half-baked loaf with—write *what*
boy?   and i'm obliged to come clean and render
unto caesar   —*n-novels Highness, n-namas and whatnot.*

—ah! a *nov*-e-list! well, well! a big time spender!
had I but known there'd be another door
bricked up here, and signposted, what's more:

RETURNED TO SENDER.

*U*pon *which the Ghost vanishes leaving Irv shaken. But one man
knows the purple cure.*

the little finger of his Majesty's left hand
defies the stoutest sword arm in the land—
then how much mightier yet the royal tongue,
yea, than a damascus sword!
the ink pen trembles to record
the merest smitch his daily words among

Abu'l Fazl, p.m.

heart-ravishing sayings of HM

- absolute zero is wider than true north by half.

- true north is farther than a neighbour's wife.

- a neighbour's ox eats twice the measure of thine own.

- east is east but measure your bread by the baking stone.

- people in stone houses should not glaze to the south.

- the stolen mango is sweetest in a drought.

- east is south when the world leans on its elbow.

- the former light of the world got off his tiger (aiyyo).

- the paper dragon should beware the candle by the bed.

- in the country of the toothless is the best head.

- better a stale fish fry than a bad ghazal.

- [*conjec.*] this poet's a right pain in the abu'l fazl.

- neither can i (haha). *

*dismissing the following claim of grounds for divorce:
M-Majesty, she can't sleep with the light on, i can't read in the dark.

The Ghost returns to the Court of Public Audience, the Diwan-i-am. His haughty mien proclaims Akbar the Great—*as if* Akbar *did not already mean* great. *The Great the Great sits in state.*

ashoka

the great? don't make Me laugh.
graffiti artist. planted six trees by
the roadside. dug a watertank or two, and said love
one another. or was that the other guy?

When close behind the Great the Great appears another courtier, Irv's own Dad.

doppelganger

he's juggling oranges
as the light gladdens.
two in the air (i'm still not sure) one
        in hand.

the hand that rubbed out pain
so you could watch
with closed eyes the headache
        slip away.

it's not his ghost.
he's alive and well and living in england,
so this can only be a double,
        irv senior.

the old man i see once every other year
and every time
i pick up pliers, wrench or drill, or
        do chambers,

the dictionary, not the law.
suspect the wrong suspect, being suspicious,
clip a mad eyebrow, or
        startle awake.

i have his copshop relics handy.
arrowheads from an archery fad, spent ammunition
casings, brass calendar with ebonite stand,
        a sphinx

with staring eyes,
day and month cards gone,
but the date drum still rolls when you twist
        its ears.

another twist, it shows the two black eyes
i gave it fifty years ago
when he frowned and kept his counsel.
        still does.

he's let go one orange as the light dims down,
and—as it falls—i see the trick lies in
how daily, invisibly, the good unsex
        the great.

I had a father too, Irv, *Zelaldinus Claudius seems to say*—don't we all—and *(growing pensive)* my father a father before him, first Mughal.

Sir, *says Hamlet Irv.*

babur's grave

high on the wooded hill
the grave overlooks Kabul.

how long have i stood rapt
in this foxed plate

from some childhood book?
pine needles underfoot.

gunfire from quite near.
your life taught only lulls in war,

said, paradise
is nowhere if not here.

Zahir-ud-din Muhammad Babur (1483-1530), founder of the Mughal
dynasty.

humayun

bookish, myopic. saddled
with a darling sporty

father. his chances further addled
by a feted son. at thirty

misplaces a kingdom. spends
his best years flogging raffle

tickets in iran. ends
back in power, snaffle

and curb intact, horse gone.
shoehorned

in somehow, footing at last secure, when
dreaming one day (still in colour, now in persian)

he falls from his library stair.
halfway down the wind changes,

                                                          air

catches him up to lay him gently down
under our finest dome.

fate's clown
come home.

Nasir-ud-din Muhammad Khan Humayun (1508-1556), second Mughal
emperor.

Babur, Humayun, Akbar, the Mughal line runs. Up next, HM seems to want a laud.

Our *finest* dome, Irv? *He temporizes.* Finer than my grandson's Taj Mahal?

Surely, Sir, *answers Irv.* In Agra it's *your* tomb I visit, at Sikandra.

Sovereignty's a strange thing, Irv, *HM observes, relenting.* Some of it's luck, some audacity, some just repetition that by its nature binds, so lame you want to scream. But its panoply secures you, spans like concrete the yawning gulf, the way you lid a septic tank. Lime, shingle, gravel, 1:2:7, mesh of rebar, keeps you hung. Less will hang you. Part reach, part grasp, it scorns the muck below. You're in it anyway, anon, but best keep out while living, reigning anyway.

The Crown of India

God's in his heaven, George on the throne. 1911.

Large parts of the globe are pink, large parts will soon be red. Sikri hill always was.

In London a masque, *The Crown of India*, music by Sir Edward Elgar, his Op. 66, opens at the Coliseum to commemorate the Delhi Durbar. A rambling plot reminds the audience masque is spectacle: procession of Mogul kings, dance of the nautch girls. Blonde Nancy Price, soprano, is India, Agra a notable contralto.

Sikri doesn't feature, but Irv googles all the same to check on George and Mary+India+royal+itinerary. Search engines would severely try Edwardian belief, their future all tubes and suction cups. Always we bark up the wrong tree.

Irv retiles the powder room at Sikri station, shakes out the mattresses in Lord Curzon's lodge just in case. In fact the royals skip even Agra and the Taj, go hunting in Nepal instead. Sikri returns to waiting.

Long after Akbar a minor Mughal got himself crowned here.

But in London massed choirs rend the Coliseum sky. The afternoon of Empire began at intermission and no one knows it. Or why would Elgar so lightly cede his elegiac note?

The panegyric's an underrated form, Irv, wouldn't you say?

Sir, *says Irv, immune to barefaced angling.*

A courier enters with an envelope for the King, who signs for it to be opened. It's a marriage proposal from one, Ms. N. Price, India.

Will no one rid me of this meddlesome creature? *HM sighs.*

Distrusting a Ghost who blows now hot now cold, Irv buttons his lip and withdraws, backing out of the Diwan-i-am.

At the Tumblers' Gate he glances by way of farewell at the bricked-up door, that narrowly escaped fate, and slips out by a portal known today only to gardeners and garden lizards.

t rex

this dun stealth across gravel
is lizard,

stalking elastic garden hose,
no kin.

he creeps up to the coil
and stops

does a slowed down mating dance
of two

sinewy pressups and straightoff
kisses

the chaste extruded rubber lip
dispensing

drop by drop the only
diamonds

in this abandoned court of kings.

he sips
then seems to eat nature's hardest thing,

champing
each dazzling mouthful, this mesozoic

chieftain
who turns to face me when i move

and tilts
his head one degree or sixty

million years
to look at the lapsarian world

of giant
volvo buses, danes, and touts

and me,
his Akbar

to a *t.*

in camera

looking up i find i've stepped
into a stranger's photograph

i go obediently into that jail
to pass at length

on good behaviour
into the c.d. of her travels.

how often have i played
this walk-on part,

snapped, not known
however briefly

in this dead city where cameras
complete the kill.

she might have paused,
i might have sketched her back,

uncovered some province
of six or eight strokes

where   we overlapped,
not in the finished lines but

in the boundless moment
of their making.

old sikri road

and then i'm on the bus
home,   a rattletrap whose plexiglass
slides back to admit whole pages of mughal dust

bound up with air. sky vast as a volvo windscreen,
trees slant as volvo wipers, wicking away
the slightest breath of moisture from the earth.

sun diamantine.
glass foreedge acid green.
across the road canary yellow

caterpillar trucks build the new highway to sikri.
men in fizzyorange vests bend over
dumpy levels triangulating what's to come,

the past a figment.
right then it heaves up like a galleon—
an Akbar milestone!

househigh reliquary stupa
housing nothing more sacred than
an armpit hair

shed by some harassed mason of Zelaldinus' day.
and suddenly I see
the whole unbroken series stretch

kos by *kos*
back to the empire's zero milestone,
that extravagantly tusked tower outside his elephant gate.

sikri folk still use the cowmile,
gaukos, as a handy reckoning (within earshot
of the lowing of a cow) and I want

to yell (or low) out to my king
(from the depths of that animated
waiting on a once and future father

that is everyman's estate)   *Jal-al-ud-din!   Zel-al-din-us!*

but my own old man hears me better when
i don't shout—and so do i.

WINTER

Winter in Sikri is no less cruel than summer. Smoke from a hundred braziers stings the pilgrim's eye. Drawn back to Akbar's dead city, Irv pulls his shawl close about his shoulders at the saint's tomb early one January morning.

the saint wakes

cold in the ground
cold above it

cold at the white tomb's marble lattice
cold in the cirrused upper air

cold in the slattern swift's nest
(always good once for an egg
fried straight on red rock)

cold in the bone's shadow
cold in the close embrace of regret
centuries contemplating mightily
all I might have done
or done otherwise

mostly you miss earth's beauty
see where the morning mist defrocks the egret
watch it ghost the flying shuttlecock

what wouldn't i give for a hot game of badminton
with the petty bourgeoisie
of this flyblown town
with vulgar trishul vipul on curzon's lawn

just once to tread
grass under bare foot

too long in your swoon lord
too long disembodied

give me
me back

the ghost walks

Irv! You're back.

Majesty! [*shuffling*] I couldn't keep away.

Count your blessings, Irv. *I* can't bear to stay. I just overheard my saint beg to be re-embodied and thought—Yesss!

[*They sit on a culvert by the ticket gate*]

Listen, you're a storyteller. You can embody me. I'm sorry I was rude about your profession. Some of my best friends are novelists now—a Senegalese, a Kiwi. But they all go home. I can't go past that *gate!* Come on, embody me, walk me away. I've been too long on this hill.

[*Irv considers*] There *is* a remedy, Majesty. But it's worse than the disease—or more final.

Nothing could be worse, Irv.

You'll have to do as I say, Your Highness. The way my characters do.

Done, says Zelaldinus.

It's not just your characters that obey you when you write, Majesty. The whole world does. In that sense—begging your pardon—I'm more absolute a monarch than You.

Ahem, says Zelaldinus.

A mountain *is*, when I say so on the page. A gun goes off when I pull a trigger that wasn't there before.

Remember I can't write.

Narrate, then. Declare. Command. Say: 'Leaves appear on this bare branch.'

That smacks of heresy, Irv.

It's the only way out of here—if You really want that.

More than anything, Irv.

Story yourself out then. Say 'Zelaldinus walks down the Sikri road.'

Are you sure about this? I won't be struck down? Okay. 'Zelaldinus walks down the Sikri road.' What's this? [*bridles, rears up*] What's happening to me!

[*calls after him*] You're walking down the Sikri road. Like You said.

[*calls back*] I can't go like this, Irv! I'm not *dressed*, for one. And I need ostriches and eunuchs and things.

Create them—but then You'd be back where You started. This is something You have to do alone, Majesty.

Stop me, Irv!

Stop Yourself. Say, 'Akbar halts.'

'Akbar halts! Akbar halts! Akbar halts!'

Just the once. You've stopped.

Have I? Why, yes I have. 'Akbar returns,' then.

There, You've got the hang of it.

Look, Irv. Can't you embody me in one of *your* stories?

What sort of story?

Oh passion, romance. An old man needs a love story.

[*Irv sighs*] Alright. Listen. Here are two lovers. See them?

No.

Okay. Here's Percival.

Something moved, Irv—just there!

Percival of Bombay.

Yes—he's taking shape!

Um, maybe wipe Bombay. Another *bhel puri* blockbuster and I'll puke. Percival of Cal.

You mean Kolkata? Some pukesome stuff there, Irv.

Cal, not Kol. Percy's an Anglo. Free School, no ropetrick, no arselick. In love with, let me see, a *Paki*!

I like this game, Irv.

Well don't tell the saint about it. Okay, let's see. Visa problems! She's stuck there, he's stuck here. Karachi, Cal. They've had just one night together at a conference in, oh, Seoul. Now they're sure this is it.

She needs a name, Irv.

Patience? An Anglo too. Or no, we'll make her a Parsi. Percy's Parsi. We'll call her Naz.

Nice name, Naz.

Crush from Delhi University days, Sir. So, Percy and Naz. We have to get them together. His applications turned down twenty times, Percy decides the only way is—what?

Easy peasy, Irv. He can *walk* across.

Yes, Sir! But he could get lost. He needs a guide, someone who's been that way, done the route.

That could be me, Irv.

Majesty.

percy

perce stands north of tall. assam tea skin
hair cut rough
pushed back with long fingers. chin

he neglects to shave.
overlap to the upper lip a pout shared
with the paddyfish. brave

attempt at beard.
steady eyes.   class three
dental occlusion. build able bodied.

cal knows no cold: he's come up
country unprepared, is wearing all his tees together
under the smoky shawl he picked up

by the bus stand, so three colours, payne's
grey, white, and red, ring his neck. when his crimson balaclava
crests sikri ridge he's like the sarus crane,

tallest flighted bird. straggler of the flock. hostage
to love, grounded for now.
sparing of verbiage.

confession

Father Monserrate in black cape and biretta is pacing below the women's quarters, practising restraint. His alabaster earlobes glow with the effort. He writes to Rome with one gaunt finger in the frosty air.

'I fully believe the King inclines
towards our faith
and lacks but a dram
of persuasion to turn altogether
to the one true god.
Your grace may expect results
by *[tick one]*
march/ july/ september/and by'

[When suddenly a young man treads on his cassock]

Where to in such haste, my son?

[Perce has an open book in his hand] Sorry, good Father. Can you guide me to the watergate?

And what's your business there?

Curiosity, Father.

A tourist?
Yes, Father, housed at the ASI bungalow here.

Lord Curzon's folly! Ah well, the Archaeological Survey do some good.

The guidebook mentions a *nooria*—an aqueduct.

A nooria! Why, we had those at home. This one is of his Majesty's devising. But the watergate is bricked up. Only such as I can enter there. Follow this wall if you must—but not as far as the zenana, for that way lies temptation.

I'll keep clear, Father, and come back for confession, if that's all right.

Your mind is troubled, son?

A little, Father.

You burn?

I burn Father. For every beauty, truth be told. But I'm lost to one across the border.

What border, child?

With Pakistan.

A country, then?

Our enemy, they say. Yet the only one of theirs I ever met I loved.

Who is this child, my son?

A Paki, Father, born and bred.

And what is she to you?

No relation, good Father, but promise of bliss.

Where does she live?

In Karachi, Father.

And where is that?

The wrong side of the track. Twenty visa applications have come back.

Yet you have met?

Online, good Father.

Ah yes, I know of that. And you chatter daily?

[with dignity] Chat, Father. Nightly.

These meetings have always been, how shall I say, virtual?

Sadly, Father.

Be it so until the nuptial day. Go in peace, my son.

[Perce returns after some time] Walled up, as you say, Father. Will you confess me now? Two riders, Father:

a) it wasn't *wholly* virtual, and

b) I cannot hate a Paki.

Come back to me for the first. b) is in Caesar's domain. The court
of public audience lies that way. Do your obeisance to the King
and ask his counsel. You have a petition?

I have a ticket.

Let me see. *[examines it]* Well, go join the throng in the Diwan-
i-am. This noon the King judges—or rather Hiran, his elephant
does—criminals. So beware! There's a stone hassock below the
throne where you must on *no* account rest your head.

Best go early with the civil suitors. Here is some Europe
petitioner. Follow him.

Zelaldinus sits in state.

'Princes, Guards, Executioners, Courtiers, Fan Bearers, Ladies, Attendant Syce, Litter Bearers, Heralds, Trumpeters, etc.' on loan from the London Coliseum, strut about the terrace below the throne.

In the great courtyard beyond mill a thousand petitioners.

Irv ushers a party to the front of the queue.

the china poets

the china poets have come to do you homage, King,
renewing ancient vows between our nations.

two rivers run in ouyang jianghe's name.
he wept before your grandson's taj mahal.
see river-river's cupped hands brim with marble

tears. the night cricket accompanies xi chuan's high keening,
adding our native erhu to a fisherfolk song
that yangtze and yamuna may flow cordially

together. watch zhai yongming unseam from this lump
of szechuan coal a white chrysanthemum,
as ge fei microblogs a sikri eulogy.

old li tuo puddled concrete for the chairman in '66,
skimming off that flinty broth sublime reflections.
bei dao spreads for Your Majesty's foot

a leather jerkin from that moment after tiananmen
when poets were rockstars. these trifles
and their whole art they offer with clean hands.

now watch this monkey snatch the glasses
off my nose as the china poets look on. from roof
to roof it runs. I never thought to see clear again, Majesty

but a banana coaxed it down. today we stand united
before Your throne, eyes shut against the blinding light,

an inch between us and the redstone floor

House them in the Rose-scented quarters, *Zelaldinus commands, turning to the next petitioner.*

Enter in buskins Terence Golightly, English gentleman.

golightly

Madgesty i be terence golightly, gentylman
walked from england to see Thee.

bearing no needless bounty from my quean,
no gaudy jewell, no trumpery,
naught but a yeoman hearte gode keen
to plant before thyself on bended knee.

once robbed, twyce beaten, left for dead,
relieved of camera digitalis withal, his
collar no lytle motheaten, his cod
peece the worse for daily goad, nathless

your servaunt remaineth of gode
chere. and hath moreover ytales to tell
of wonders met upon the road.
eke a proven alchemycall yspell

for spagyric extracture of gold
from straw. wherefore he beggeth
hospitality and wode make bold
(ere forlorn home he leggeth,

his lonley planyt bosom-clutcht)
to narrate by strenuous mime
hairraising tales new-snatcht
from wanderyngs outlandish and sublyme.

a game of bowles he hath already taught
involvyng bat and wickets three
(being exercizd of sweaty sport)
to twice eleven yong roisterers of siquiri.

no missionarie he. enthuziast rather
of gastronomie, meanyng to convert
this nacion onlie to such repast
as pease parritch, spotid dyk, and toat

in the hole. wherefore gode King in goddes name,
the Great, the merciful who shines alike
on Besse and Uqbar of commensurate fame,
grant shelter to this pallid tyke,

els he wode no option have but
to figure smalle in bollyewode
playing seconde soldier tommy redcote,
or lecherous teaplanter spode.

the bat and boots, Sir, publicans of noat,
display the shoon he wore down from the holy land,
and shold his talent, albeit some whitt pedestryan,
serve but Your Madgesty one moat,

herewyth terence golightly at Your fote.

After Thomas Coryate, who walked from London to India in Shakespeare's
day. He was walking back when dysentery waylaid him. He lies buried in
Surat.

Tarry a while, Gulli, *says Zelaldinus.* We might have need of thee.

Golightly withdraws.

Percy, up next for audience, remembers too late the myrobalan comfits Irv recommended for a gift.

giftless

no gift*!* *hm hm*—HM observes and calls
for his pet elephant, hiran. *contrite*
or not, just lay your head, young percival,

upon this granite hassock at my feet—no wait!
i shout—*you shut up, irv*—but lightning rod
percy's already on the ground prostrate,

his head upon the rock, as at the royal nod
hiran lifts one great pestle foot—
when slugabed perce leaps up in time untrod

upon, and percival the almost late
but seldom shiftless parries
why Sir! *freedom's* your gift—beyond that gate.

the touch

so red records and this black button takes you home
—Zelaldinus mutters, slipping percy's ipod
touch into his placket. then briskly—*come*

clean, boy, what drives the thing? my lord
says perce—through clenched teeth—a tiny cell.
then step this way, consider this scrimshawed

engine here.* observe. your coin dings in this well,
rolls down a race, strikes twenty pins, then this green
parrot pops up here, pecks this ace infidel

who frights this cat, which quits the scene
by this nether flap to teeter afterwards
up here (same cat? another?) where, inclined to preen,

it overturns a dish of curds
onto this english lord, who stamps
your weight and fortune on two cards.

—*your coin?* and percy resolutely champs
the royal bit, unpurses, rolls hapless eyes,
and renders up his rupiyah. Akbar decamps.

thus does a printer's 'prentice subsidize
(as scripture prophesies a common man
redeem) the emperor of all hindoostan.

'[I]n one chamber the Armenian interloper distracts HM with fanciful
devices in deplorable taste …'

Abu'l Fazl, p.m.

hardware

my hall of engines, perce,
the imperial workshop. just shy
of my heir apparent's talkshop. here
we teach the hardest trick of all

in this touch-we-not land.
how goods are brought to be. here
prod the cogs of industry. temper meteorite
steel for an axletree. true waterwheels

with a simp1e cotter pin (ask my firstborn
what a cotter pin is, haha). this here's
the gunnery, that's ordnance,
refrigeration here, looms there.

lace, pottery, dyeing, footwear.
prince's first shoe looking for a last,
haha. through there's china. the country, not
the pot. look at them. yes, they went

overboard, broke heads, neglected verse,
but sent every last ragpicker's child to a
school like this or gave her a violin.
lunch thrown in. sign at our back door

says *NOT BY SOFTWARE ALONE*. truth
be told, perce, it was not your line
about the gate that cheated hiran. just
the line of dirt under your nails.

'He has built a workshop near the palace where are studios and workrooms
for…painting, goldsmith work, tapestry-making, carpet and curtain-
making, and the manufacture of arms.'

Father Antonio Monserrate

'The next moment he would be seen shearing camels, hewing stones,
cutting wood, or hammering iron.'

Pierre du Jarric, SJ, missionary

Houose the boy in Lord Curzon's lodge, *says Zelaldinus,* and the other in a camel chimney.

And this is your lady love? *He's already learnt to call up photos.*

Sir, *answers Percy, warily. He's read about seignorage and a lord's first rights to any bride.*

Never fear, boy. Tell me all, *Akbar commands, and Percy narrates the story of Naz.*

Sindh is now in Pakistan?

Sadly, *says Percy.*

I happen to have been born there, Percy.

And as Zelaldinus' eyes mist over Percy takes heart.

first kisses

first kisses, Majesty,

you remember them?

of course you do.

what's four hundred years?

nocturne

Nightshawled Percival crosses the Diwan-i-am. That great
courtyard black as tank water. The palace wall stalks him in
silhouette, its colonnade the legs of some creature that stops
every time he turns to look. Gingerly he steps through the
chained gate. Sikri hill peters out here, the Agra road sloping
down and away along its spine through the old imperial market.
Percy heads for the ASI bungalow. His boots spank gritty
echoes off the verandah walls, the drum house a brooding tower
wreathed in mist beyond. He has Lord Curzon's suite.
Naubat Singh peon has laid a second quilt on the bed.

Instantly asleep, he wakes to a hand at his throat—three t-shirts
ridden up together around his neck—and lies there panting. Two
skylights, like TV screens high up in the opposing wall, show
a dressing-gowned figure pacing on the terrace roof. Smoke
flowers at the petalled chimneypots where the wraith tilts a
watering can. Sootblack petunias, limewhite periwinkle nod.
Lord Curzon's pate a risen moon.

Down climbs the ghost, sits, pulls on bedsocks. *My* bed, he pops
his eyes at Percy.

Percy takes up the top quilt and tramps downhill. A shape rears
up out of the shadows and spits through rotten teeth—*Password*?

He answers—*Naz*—and the weather turns delicate.

A night market by glowworm light. Embroidered shoes clapped
in the air, purslane fritters held out on a slotted spoon. Perce

burns his tongue, cools it on crushed green ice. The stump of an arm is thrust in his face; he balances a small coin on the crusted bandage. The former pickpocket shows him the bones of his foot against a slab of pitchblende. In the next stall blue starfish from Yemeni waters doze in a ring of torchlight. A racoon fidgets on a leash, turns a nervous eye on the procuress who murdered his Quebecois master. Perce bends over her quicksilver basin where the last customer's image still quakes. *Sumptuous!* the lecher breathes his last as a bolt of mauve taffeta falls from his hands. *Thrown away!* is the coral merchant's lament—*tomorrow we starve!* His podgy godson giggles. Satin stoles snap at Percy's calves. Crocheted caps flap in his face. A hag presses a brass key into his palm and shambles off. Boy hawkers of dill must move on before the stalls of jealous merchants who stock crystal urns, brocade, and toothpicks of moot gold. At the bottom of the hill, beyond the tinsmith's tattoo and the pyramids of onions, turbits in their slate and tan cravats prink before cage mirrors. The pigeon-sellers are farthest from the palace for the stink. *Guttergoo, guttergoo,* a Mauritian pink coos, rubbing its gorget against the skylight pane.

Perce wakes in his bed, to tea and scorched bread. Pantry Naubat has fetched real butter on a bicycle from the old town.

Expecting a crust, forepaws trembling on the doormat, a metis wolfhound duchess.

Beneath her claws, a letter.

letters (2)

i go
to put

the buttered
toast down

but see
her paki

letter there
and   hesitate

then do
it anyway.

the censors
(theirs and

ours) weren't
virginal, so

what's another
franking?

            there!

love's   strait.

            there,there,there,there,there

lovesarchipelago.

letters,   like
love, improve

by staining.

naz waiting

the pumpkin on the roof
holds its breath
      (i led the vine up here)

jehangir's car seat (he'll lend us his jalopy) awaits your bum
mrs q's gatelatch your hand
and the squeak in the gatelatch

this peeling window waits
and its shadow on the wall
the cool china insulators in the fuse box
pipes full of fresh water

a fridge full of food for our siege
new peppercorns packed in a perspex mill
crock of jackfruit pickle
edam snug in its red balaclava
king oscar sardines
one bottle of still mustard oil
(a year of karachi afternoons)

the bedroom ceiling fan poised like a runner on his starting
blocks
white cotton sheets smoothed to distraction
the space in between them

               a refinery exploding

and one stopped lover
a clock waiting

for time to begin

i am the emperor

torpid as a swift in winter,
prone in spring to laxity.
migrating always further hinter,
i am the prince of accidie.

she (and she, and she) is mine to
hold. crossed, i turn curmudgeon.
operatics i incline to,
i am the emperor of dudgeon.

i scan the ceiling for her phantom:
not there—not there—not there—not there.
set to pick a straw at random,
i am the emperor of despair.

goosefleshing at the slightest sound
—lord curzon's ghost last night—
loitering, not karachi bound,
i am the emperor of fright.

a railway closet so revolts me,
i, who'd do the least thing for her,
would shunt her off if she should goad me.
i am the emperor of horror.

nothing stares back where i stand,
blank space in the luscious mirror.
nothing lifts an empty hand,
i am the emperor of terror.

but let one pale green postpaid paki
envelope slip into sight,
helot in luck's hierarchy,
i am the emperor of delight.

the well

dug
by
a
man
who
plaits
a
rope
of
grass
and
winds
it
round
and
round,
shoring
up
the
earth
walls
as
he
goes,
and
when
he's
gone

you're
let
down
ankle
roped
to
dangle
swaying
upside
down
voiding
your
head,
one
with
the
dark,

turning.

Akbar too is vacillating. He's revived his old practice of meditating suspended by his feet in a well.

'Time, Sir,' *Percival calls down the shaft.*

That evening he stands on the roof of the ASI lodge above the twinkling lights of Sikri village. From the servants' quarter carries the high brooding voice of Naubat's wife.

sikri lullaby

do you never go beyond the mesh on your cradle.
do you never go beyond the slats on your cot.
do you never go beyond this threshold with the bolthole.
do you never go beyond the elephant gate.
do you never go beyond naubat's hailing.
do you never go beyond chapter five.
do you never go beyond the knot of her drawstring.
do you never go beyond one wife.
do you never go beyond six daughters.
do you never go beyond the khyber pass.
do you never go beyond the black waters.
do you never go beyond the moon's broad face.
do you never go beyond the hem of god's garment.
and i will love you all my days.

trains

what are trains like, perce?
        asks the King.
they glide like etiquette, Sir,
through halls of protocol,
flash past liquid crystal lights, draw up at distant portals
in cities of plate glass,
and never stop for ordinary mortals.
        trains are class.

what are trains like, percival?
        asks monserrate.
they glide like grace, father,
on rails that meet at the horizon.
all who ride them must show a dispensation that says shriven
or face eternity in prison.
they never stop till they arrive in heaven.
        trains are extreme unction.

what are trains like, farsi?
        asks the saint.
they jolt like disillusion, baba,
board them with caution.
and should you begin to enjoy the ride it's just temptation.
get off and walk no matter if you're sick or well
for the next stop is damnation.
        trains are hell.

i'll tell you what trains are, mr percy,
          says general man singh.
they glide like vultures, mr percy.
bars on the windows, blood on the track,
convoy of carrion crows cross-dressed in black,
dead guard in the last carriage
who never stops to pick up widows.
          trains are carnage.

what are your trains like, perce?
          asks naz.
they ride like skin on skin, woman
like ours that night.
no different from your trains really, same green flag, same red
light,
same shitty toilet, same unchanging fare,
same penalty stop chain.
          trains get you there.

then *why* do they stop at the border, percy?
says percy's woman.
ask the border guards, woman. buggered if i know why they stop
at the border.
          planes are better.

last cup of tea with a sadhu at sikri truckstop

luck against you, your eyes say.
no, my friend, i'd say greatly *for,* this far.

you get the midrange most days.
be grateful there's no one minding the shop.

i'd say go fetch her.
before she's married off to some old lecher.

but get a job—
love and fresh air won't do.

in my day you clogged the civil service or went into tea.
better a life in onions, i thought. pushcart under the sky, gliding

the long gradients, street ballet.
but the same shirt every morning shouts poverty.

rich is better, like the lady said.
i'd go with you

but last night on the open road the owl circled over me,
returning for a second look

and anyway the king's good company.
how was the tea?

good, says percy, his mind made up.
allow me.

and dreadlocked ash-smeared irv, who never had a son, winces
and lets him pay.

future perfect

tense immaculate.
i will have caught

up.
fire.
a fine fish.
as catch can.
my death of cold if I wait here any longer.
the 5.22 to karachi.

exodus

They say Fatehpur Sikri ran out of water. But some claim the King lost interest in a city once new and intoxicating. Others speak of an epidemic that emptied its lanes. Some hint darkly at a crisis of faith. Still others say the death of Tansen left a gap through which the Emperor slipped away.

How then did Fatehpur Sikri end?

The truth is a small brown coin disappeared from circulation.

A coin hardly noticeable in the palm. Yet it passed through every hand. Rake, godman and wick-trimmer, all at one time looked through the hole at its centre.

It must be said at once that no specimen of this coin has been unearthed at Mughal or higher levels. But the evidence points to a sudden decline in its value. It appears all classes came to hoard a substance whose life lay in its circulation. Henceforth all transactions were measured in silver, trust at a premium. Since the exchange rate of the metal now exceeded the nominal value of each unit the coin was everywhere melted down.

Presently not a single specimen remained.

Sikri was doomed. One by one its brightest jewels dimmed. Save one whose name for cunning will live forever. Far into the future, Birbal will survive.

Amar Chitra Katha

birbal and the poor widow's safe

he adjusts his boson earphone implant.

slides open the widow's xpotentio bay and scans the
motherboard. not there.

in the cellar he checks the drawer of her pepper mill, fetching a
deep nostalgic breath.

on sudden inspiration he throws open the antique mesh foodsafe.
seizes a jam jar and holds it to the light.

brazen!

suspended in the golden gel among the gooseberries and their
tiny interplanetary seeds it hangs like a starship.

the failsafe key.

he empties the jar onto the selenite benchtop. sucks the key
clean and licks his fingers fastidiously. chews to pap a slice of
white bread. pats the mash around the key and swallows it.

for a long time the spycam must watch his front teeth worrying a
gooseberry seed.

<*too sweet*> the only audio snatch.

keystone

every morning in fatehpur sikri the masons of the a.s.i secretly
remove a series of weathered stones.

in a workshop below the palace wall each stone is faithfully
replicated

in the image of the ideal ancestor.

every afternoon the new pieces are cunningly cemented back in.

when a fresh piece is lodged a suspect piece beside it is marked.

exact copies of stone latticework are inserted where worn ones
hung.

stone by stone

building by building

the palace is renewed.

likewise the gardens, parterre by parterre.

water channel and fountain are miraculously restored.

on the hillside stand the remains of noblemen's mansions.

whole walls in these structures that once were derelict are patiently
rebuilt.

where brick or rubble was used instead of stone, brick or rubble are
used.

the mortar corresponds to a medieval recipe stated in the *ain-i-Akbari,*

three parts of gravel to one of lime, with brick dust and molasses mixed in.

but there remain certain mysteries and unattainables.

the caterpillar struts are a mystery.

the barleysugar pillars imponderable.

among things that cannot be duplicated

the great squinchnet beehives one hundred and twenty feet up in

the arch of the victory gate,

cell upon cell of sculpted wax.

at the end of each day's work the tailings mount up

forming a scree that slopes up to the ramparts

by which the brigand can climb up to the fortress by night.

piece by piece he too plunders the palace.

in the forest department this attrition is called mortality.

but fatehpur sikri is already dead.

the archaeological survey of india accepts this truth.

philosophically it implants stone after stone

upto the keystone itself

till a perfect replica stands on sikri hill

and nothing remains of Zelaldinus' city

except the idea of it.

setting out

—*pace all that, percy,* says Akbar, popping
up in the autorickshaw, *we're off!*   the a.s.i's
stone bungalow and arty chimneys dwindling

as pantry naubat and wife wave fond goodbyes,
and the duchess, couchant in a monumental sulk,
refuses to so much as lift her eyes.

ages since I ventured past the agra gate, that hulk
in the distance. but tell Me, what's it like out there?
I need a change of air. well, Sir, in the bulk

the mode of production's changed. despots i dare
say are no thinner on the ground. but there's a crew
who lead us, voted in and out, a fair

constitution, a supreme court, two
houses for lawmakers, a new nation
across the border (actually a few).

overall less plunder, more placation.
there's been a trickledown. take your Shahinshah's
larder. today a man of middle station

can manage gorgonzola, custard apples, jars
of neem honey, arabian dates, smoked salmon.
no peacock's tongues, true, but caviars—

a *middle* class man! imagine (barring famine)
the grand web of it, the sheer effrontery:
Your royal kitchen, your icerunners, outrun

by commerce. look, take a short run. come with me.
—*but my fellow passengers, won't they be common?*
and perce rolls a canny eye at His Majesty.

every train has one superb uncommon woman.
she is always across the aisle, and she will
stay on the train when you get off, or if you stay on

—she'll get off. this is law. and as a codicil
she'll slip into a sweater just when
her naked arm achieves perfection, though you'd kill

for her. true, these laws apply to all men,
including Emperors.—*ah, perce, end of parlay,*
here's where I get off, call me a saracen,

(the mode of production having changed, per se).
go on then, boy. goad that engine driver
as we do all creatures. go get her, percy.

Cursing the King for a coward, Percy, makes his way to the border alone. In a small town by the Rann of Kutch he sits down to breakfast at a roadside eatery. He hasn't slept well and he's overcome by the unfairness of his situation.

why not now?

take an ordinary pair
of lovers.   separate us.

daily we fade
without promise of dailiness.
nightly we sleep
with this rusted fence in between.

what keeps it there?
the lives lost keeping it?

but suppose the lives were earnest money put down,
the debts cleared once and for all?

if both sides simply got up
and walked across,
tens, hundreds of thousands,
in those numbers who would stop them?

              and after the mend you simply—go to peshawar!
no here, no there,
the border a line of weeds.

trains buses tempos every day.
dailydailydaily the man at enquiries is tired of explaining.

the boys on the roof not fleeing,
the knife in the satchel a fruit knife.

ropes of figs their garlands.

it's some way off.
it's also very close.   smell it.

it   is   very   close.

take one breath, stop all talk
and walk.

*P*ercy's bun omelette arrives just as his eye catches the headline on his neighbour's paper.

PAK WONT BLINK. INDIA FIRM. N-ARSENALS ON RED ALERT.

Naz! He must get there at once. Let them perish together in Karachi.

At length his thoughts slope back to Irv and the King on Sikri hill.

black wind

black city
inside the red.

silence cools
off total heat

palm trees
bent over

hair flung
all one way

a row of vultures
vapoured

darkness fingers
the harem

black curdles
where cells

had notions.
your jaw

rang Sir
when that

matchlock jammed.

just gunpowder.

now look.

red and black
gone white

ash quilts
sikri hill

the boy
leaping into

the moat
for that

small coin
evaporates

falling into
no reflection

The man on the next bench lowers his paper.

Makes no sense to me, boy.

No sense at all, *Percy replies.* It's all one country. Always was.

No, I mean this paper. I still can't read. *He takes off his dark glasses.*

Sir! *Percy chokes. It's the King!*

You didn't think I'd leave you in the lurch, did you Percy?

crossing the line

If nine out of ten living creatures live in the sea and not one
in ten land creatures lives in this salt waste, life is—what—a
hundred times more precious here than anywhere else on the
face of the earth? wonders Percy as he scans the seesawing Rann
of Kutch. The King in unsteady outline on another camel up
ahead calls back.

Give Me an elephant any day, Perce.

The noncommittal horizon rocking black and silver in the night.

Give me even Indian Airlines, Sir.

You have to hand it to Golightly though. He got Me here.

That shape to the south is not a phantom tree but Golightly on
his grey camel. He waves and turns away. He has an appointment
with dysentery in Gujarat.

The King frowns at the map Percy handed him when their
camels conferred. The alleged road does not exist. Or once did
and has been swallowed up. Or He's holding the map upside
down. Or the day's glare got to Him.

He can't dismiss that vision of white windmills by the sea,
turning silently.

The camels keep bearing north towards the sands. Where the ground turns marshy they fret and want to tread an invisible line between two kinds of wilderness. Northwards, the shifting sand dunes of the Thar where the wind erases every footprint before the next is made. Southwards, where long tides lap in great glass mirrors, stretches the Rann. Vast nothing on the country's flank. Grass and bush, the bustard, the wild ass, and little else living. No way across. Or ten thousand ways leading nowhere.

Last thread of moon in the sky at 5 am. Dawn is breaking.

Travel on the Rann is strictly by night so the pair call a halt and bed down for the day under cover of the only trees for miles. Three feathery grey *prosopis juliflora*. Percy's drying off, crisp and salted like a chip from a tumble taken with his only change of clothes on. When the muse transporting him suddenly bent to drink from a pool of rainwater in a cup of rock.

They're on a desert island. Firm flood-plain knoll, saltwater marooned. The encroaching sea has not yet drowned this tuffet. These stunted trees growing out of yellow rock are real, cast a luminous shade like frosted glass.

Beckoning all day long half an inch above the horizon, the false trees.

Head down, Percy drinks, no hands, where the camel drank. The puddle stills, gives back a face he blows into because a mirror in the wilderness is obscene. Looks over at the King in plain clothes, a man among men. Zelaldinus did the talking with the Rabari cameleteer, persuaded the man with a small pierced coin. Trust. Bought four blackbrush camels that belong across the border. So the beasts follow their noses back home, leaving the russet breed that keep east of the Rann. A tracker can tell Pak from Indian camels by the size of the footprint. He'd report these as wild ones of theirs that wandered down.

Two days and a night since Perce and the King quit the Badali Pir's pilgrim party and set out on their own. The border is due north here, not west. The sea a murmurous crest of surf beyond the southwest edge.

The Rann shelves out to sea for miles and twice each day the sea washes back over it leaving a new crust of white that in winter glitters like a snowfield. They lie on their backs and hear from far away a sigh that turns them on their sides to watch until a wide clear pane of water comes into view gliding in to lap at their feet on the verge of speech till the long slow suck begins again and it returns in mute obedience to the place from which it came.

Nightfall. A row of pylons stride north to south lit by the salt's gloaming.

They pass under the zinging cables, first manmade things since the tomb. Meet and cross a road running alongside the row of concrete gumboots. Demented dervish songs howl from the slung wires in the head wind. Salt gnaws at the berm pushed up by bulldozers to take a sealed road.

Next day there's a shelf of rock beside a thorn bush with some wild plum that Zelaldinus smacks out of Perce's hand just short of his mouth. The Light of the World hobbles four beasts then tethers each with a clovehitch and tests the ropes for flaws. Thank god for a handy King, Perce thinks as he twists the can opener lugs around a tin of Goa sardines. The camels nibble *juliflora*.

Hm hm, the Emperor chumbles, focussed on cold fish, unmindful of vegetarian banquets past. Before the camels turned up he'd begun to contemplate a sea crossing. Pushing off from the westernmost cape in a lifeboat. Salvaged from one of the cruise ship hulks that litter the coast. Imagine thinking they could buck the swell at the Indus creek mouths! *And* outwit two sets of coast guards without a seasoned fisherman at the till!

I hoped to show you Percy, He says shaking his head, *fresh prawns in your shoe.*

They sleep in the scant shade, a hot wind fluttering their eyelashes. Perce too is imagining those treacherous delta currents where the Indus swarms out to the Arabian Sea. He never learnt to swim. Is Plan B any safer?

The lights of Karachi effervescing on that black water, near enough to touch.

At teatime their eyes open together as a pink cloud sails overhead, honking.

The King all excited because flamingoes mean they're nearing his birthplace.

We were on the run that time too, Perce—just that way, a stone's throw from here—when I must have kicked. Mother chewed a little betel, the midwives fussing, hey? Father was informed and the palace guard spurred on to Umarkot to prepare a suite in the Raja's fort. And there I first saw light. Light this same off-yellow colour, half sand half clay, I swear.

A ghari later Perce's knuckles whiten on the handle of his mug as he sees, no honk no flutter, a galleon go sailing past their bivouac. Zelaldinus simply nods.

Mine. We sailed it downriver from Lahore to the sea. I always wanted a chunk of the Arab trade. Which other of our kings braved the deep? Our cook made seaweed bread from bladderwrack. I touched an electric eel. The river ran much further east in those days, right by here. Once we ran aground on an eyot just like this and it took a week to dig us out. The carpets drying on the thorn trees like scarlet leaves. When I was a boy in Afghanistan I learnt to love piny greens and blues but now I think this whited ochre is the ground to which all colour returns.

You know, says Percy, when the ship's gone, last night in that passing shower when it was pissing down for just two minutes I thought how nice to be a ghost and have the rain go straight through you.

No no! says the King, alarmed. *You just stay a body, Perce, or how do you expect to please young Naz across the border? Not that I mean to nose with Naz,* he grins, *but did you get on well?*

Perce's mouth goes dry at the thought of all the pleasing waiting to be done.

He crawls over to a rock pool for a drink and notices the beard the moment before it disturbs the water. She hasn't seen him any way but clean-shaven. Will there be time for a shave? Do they have roadside barbers like we do? They must—it's the same bloody country! It's then he turns sharply—droplets flying—and sees the ghost is no longer an old man. Whiskers gone black, sideburns, eyebrows, eyelashes gone back from salt to pepper. This is the King who first built himself a home on the red hill. The crown's back too.

Zelaldinus returning from a leak taken squatting behind a tussock on the other side of the mound has a new stride not sprung by bent marram grass. *Okay Perce,* He says rubbing sand between the fingers of His left hand. *We're leaving rock pools behind. This yellow flowerer's good for a drink if you're desperate. Slit the bulb like this. And mind it's not the* white *flowerer that grows beside it, or you'll be later than my late food taster.*

Now that night is falling they can risk a cratered fire and heat the leathery dalpuri pilgrim fare Zelaldinus brought and brew up real tea. But each man seems inclined to press on. The Dog Star has appeared high up in the sky and Venus down low, a quaking oyster on the horizon. They travel north all night in silence making for the Pole Star. A thousand *kos* back in Sikri say or Agra you'd have the Bear on your right. No moon tonight. The horizon this night simply a level end to stars. But starlight turns salt to snow.

An arctic waste, with camels. A greenish mantle flickers in the northern sky.

Pity you've not run guns, Percy, Zelaldinus says.

I'd have trouble running a temperature, Sir. Though at school I
ran long distance.

*You'll need that when we cross. We loose the camels on the other side.
That's when you start running. Don't stop till you reach the track.
You'll have all night. Take any train going south. That's left. I go
right, but don't wait for Me. Don't even turn round, hey?*

Then the east goes pale and it's time to find shelter. A hump
that's not soremaking and camel-black but that same Ranny
high yellow with a tree that's not mirage. Nothing offers itself
so they push on. But now risk being seen. Then another line of
pylons, strung east west this time, which means the border's just
beyond. Now they must stop, even if they spend the last day in
the open. The fence a line of rust at the horizon.

Zelaldinus makes a square of four camels on the nearest thing
to tussock, hobbling each one to the next. They bed down in the
camel coign, hardly noticing the wind that howls in their ears.
When a gust rips off the King's turban.

It goes rolling like tumbleweed beyond retrieval. *Let it go,*
Zelaldinus decrees.

Giving it hardly a glance as He slides into a bird dream. The lone bushchat that kept them company yesterday is gone.

But a harrier passes overhead silent and pale and watchful, satellite rapt. Both men follow its passage where they lie, their heads shifting by degrees.

What the satellite can't see (yet), thinks Perce, enumerating as he drops off:
Dreams. Real time misgivings. The writing on the wall. Any satellite higher than itself. Your face in my head—and then he's asleep. His head rolling off the pillow onto tiny warped tiles of crusted silt that shatter back into dust soundlessly.

Teatime again they wake to a thousand honking cranes going the other way. No water now except where the cranes were going. Each takes a small swig from the Bisleri bottle, then Perce screws the cap back on tight.

Their shadows lengthen, first bronze then violet on ash, as the sun declines. The sky goes a brief pale blue in the west and an unearthly clarity descends on the great salt pan.

Keep low, boy, Zelaldinus says. *If you look carefully beyond the power line that fuzz on the horizon isn't tree mirage. It's not mirage at all. It's fence. Barbed wire. Electrified. Look closely and you'll see the poles. Now run your eye along to where that pylon is. All right, just beside it, see that tower? That's manned. They have them every five kilometres all along the fence. Now see those taller poles? Those are floodlights, with sensors. But there's a gate in here I'm told (Birbal, who else?) where both sides do flag meetings. The only spot where*

*the razor wire stops to let you through to no man's land. In there you
don't tarry, okay? Not to read the legend on either side of the concrete
pillar, not for anything. Anyway all it says is* India *on this side and*
Pakistan *on that side. After that Umarkot's one way and Karachi the
other. You have the wirecutters? Water bottle you keep.*
We ghosts need less.

And Perce answers, Sir. His mind's already racing ahead at the
word Karachi.

That night he saw the city lights across the black water he imagined her at one of those gleams, working out in her rooftop room. Pakistan's ace hurdler. Last time they skyped she said in the sign language they've evolved she has her slow brother's passport waiting for him. The one he never used. Who says the dead are past helping us? You simply step into his shoes. And then we'll see. Madness? Yes. Madness. And then he's in that pleasing room he's yet to see.

But tell me, Perce. What was the worst thing you ever did? the King breaks in on his reverie. And Perce thinks back and says, I signed a petition to impeach a man who never hurt me. I let myself be stampeded. And at the public hearing I sneered at a man who got up and spoke fearlessly in his defence.

Zelaldinus nods. *Let go of him Perce, or he'll haunt you harder than any ghost. Abul Wasim haunts Me that way. The man whose exquisite wife I stole. And that's going back a way.*

Night falls. The Light of the World pisses the camels. They can't piss sitting so he walks them one by one, stepping back at each cascade. At midnight he counts out his Pak currency notes and gives Perce half. *From Todar Mal, our treasurer.* Not crisp, not limp, just middling. Then an attar vial from his pack. *For Naz.* He starts to sing a line in Raga Bhairavi but stops when Perce cringes. Tansen He's not. *Go serenade her, son.* Then he bows deeply: to north to south to east to west.

Now follow me. They pass under the hum of the slung cables and Perce feels a voltage in him so strong it could frizz the whole cat's cradle overhead.

Akbar holds up one hand. *Watchtower,* he whispers. Then points. *Sentry!*

Wait here, he says, *by this pylon*. And wanders off into the dark but doubles back. *Trust in god*, He whispers, *but don't forget to tie your camel. Old Turki saying*. He ties them up one by one, then sets out again. Comes up ghostwise to the man on duty who sees him—and drops, gun and all. Akbar gags and binds the sentry. Reappears at the pylon where Perce is waiting. Unties the camels and takes the halter on the leader. Now all move off together to the fence.

Wirecutters. Perce passes them.

The King cuts once, twice, three times, up and up the gate. High enough to let the camels through. *I disabled the sensors*, He whispers.

Just then the sleeping guard wakes and comes down the iron ladder. Finds his comrade trussed up on the ground. Looks at the gate. Sees them. Shouts a challenge. No answer. Starts to fire.

Run Percy! Zelaldinus shouts and Percy runs. Only one camel has got through behind him. It takes the bullets meant for him. Lies kicking in the sand as he runs. The other three bolt back onto the Rann leaving the King to absorb the hail of lead.

He takes the whole chamber muttering a mad catch with the refrain, *Go Perce!*

Men die into ghosts, ghosts have no place to go. They die back into bodies. Next morning they'll find him, more hole than body, one of the nameless dead that keep appearing on the fence. Useless bodies by a useless fence on no man's land.

Which Perce who ran at school now crosses. *Bear left,* he remembers, *or you run into a watchtower on the other side.* He runs and walks and stumbles and gets up and runs some more. All night. And at last there's the railway track. He jumps a goods train to the next station and cleans up in the bathroom. There's even a razor someone left behind. Wonders as he scrapes, did the bullets just go through like rain?

At dawn he funks the ticket window, hops ticketless on the next Karachi train.

pak train

gazing out the carriage door
green fields racing past

you are my beautiful woman

pissing down the black hole
in the squat toilet

you are my beautiful woman

eating the air? grins the railway cop
i look in his bloated face

you are my beautiful woman

SPRING

One last time the narrator returns to Fatehpur Sikri.

Masque is public utterance, admitting no private voice, but in a coda where death has emptied both citadel and narrator, Irv circles Zelaldinus' former fastness and unlocks his heart.

pilgrim days

pilgrim days at sikri.
most go on past to a desert shrine,
a stuck record, i
circle your eyrie.

six former visits spent
summer summer summer summer
winter winter.
now spring.

last assault on your citadel,
yourself no longer in to me.
a death to report and that's it
Majesty.

i don't need to go in any more,
can park the battering ram beyond the fosse.
sprawl under a centuries old plum tree, get up to piss,
lie down some more.

turn that down! the mother goddess screams
at disco bhajans turned up deafmaking high.
her votaries cup their ears at me,
what's that you say?

doppelgone

he's dead, Majesty.
guavas couldn't keep him.
he became their scent

in a room. i still can't look
at that corner of the house. it
comes closer at night.

he left by his own front door,
in a grey suit
the male nurse and i

put on him as he cooled.
in a blue tie
a neighbour from his childhood

clive road, allahabad, knotted
on his own neck then
slipped over the vacated head.

lifted into the coffin
on a sheet clammy
the day we bought it,

father
migrated from genitive
to accusative.

his ghost the column of damp
that never leaves the side
of the fridge.

do i pat it down
the way he needed,

or leave it be,
Majesty?

corms

his air horn screeches at the horizon.
the truck driver plays his scales

updowndownup updowndownup,
a riff his garage friend set up.

shred a ghost, Highness, that horn.

his red eyes ream the midnight highway,
mine rake over the red soil of this day,

unearth these corms.

I
in sikri market women from the surrounding villages shake off
their heavy tarnished silver bangles and go home decked out in
bright tin

II
a pan of sweetened milk seethes on a redstone ledge
outside a halvai's shop

above a drain where black water
stands and stinks.

arbitrating heaven and hell,
this halfhidden redstone bracket.

crusted with filth and for no earthly reason
intricately carved

III
a cloth spread on the pavement,
he empties his sack and mounds
his plums.

worked up he'd make a hill
of skulls
at the gwalior gate.

here the plum seller shapes the green hill
of his livelihood, then sits
and contemplates the way,

a desert saint

IV
on the stony path from sikri
an old man leads a billy goat,
sick or for sale or for slaughter.

assalaam alaikum i say sideways
catching up, meaning to ask him which,
but the words stick in my throat.

waalaikum salaam
he hurries to reply as i overtake them,
then returning to himself
sighs

a small highpitched cranethroated
allah!

troubles, Majesty,
a crowded plane you could steer
into a hill

V
not doors and windows any more—
the little carpenter in owly glasses smiles
the small sweet smile that everywhere
disarms civility.

that's for younger men.
now i make cots and such and get by.
today i came into town to get a new tyre.

blood-red the virgin sidewall stripe
revolves as proof

chisels in the brake bar
saw clipped at the carrier
glasses fastened with string

parting, he asks,
dovetailing the english—
sikri is *worldfamous* is it not?

when he's gone I stall in the busy road.
Majesty, is this love or what?

tree at tansen's house

tree
rooted in red rock
chain mail on the trunk
bole branching massively at ten feet
spreading by two immense outstretched limbs
through upswept grey branches
into innumerable twigs
each wicked with
a new green
flame

It was said of Tansen that his voice could light oil lamps.

on tansen's terrace at the edge of sikri hill

where the great singer sat to eat the air
i inch up to the edge
catch a breeze
that wafts up from the temple precinct

far below. four boys playing cricket there
shout first hello, then mild obscenities.
i wave, but know if all sikri were suddenly extinct
they'd push me off this ledge

for fun. i go closer, close in for the cull,
half climb half tumble down the hill,
then turn and make
through four hundred springtides for the vanished lake.

the boys are looking in the bushes for their ball.
we lose things, history loses people.
at the fence four round impassive faces follow me,

sunflowers, Majesty.

specimens

all hawks come down to this,
feathers loosed in the hollow of a hill
shared with three redstone graves under the watergate.

some battle took place here the other day.
now, among last year's leaves
and crimson oxalis spouting renewed blood,

these telltale specimens,
speckled hawkbrown,
tan, dove grey,

postcards to whom it may concern.
each spring raptor draws
raptor blood

and thrilling to the bone
soars up
to ride the thermals.

there,

circling
high above sikri hill,
the clade outriders.

patience

you finish off the mortally wounded,
this much i knew at eight.

took hold of the warm body
of the dove i'd brought down,
placed its head under my shoe
and pulled to break the neck—

but couldn't bring myself
to clamp down on the head,

that slid back out,
the small black eye still staring,
and now as well some pinkgrey down
scraped off the neck.

at which i crept away
and left the rest to fate.

*

rishab nath, first jain tirthankar,
knows about this.
reclining on the office floor
at the a.s.i. bungalow.

five hundred years his sandstone figure lay
at the bottom of a pond below this hill.

we open a window
to let in light
and find a small forgiving smile
at the corner of his mouth.

all through your masque
he held his breath, Majesty.

aliens

woman constable,
apsara in khaki, sikri girl.
stopping on her way home
to buy a cauliflower,
leaves her motorcycle helmet on.

boy from nebraska,
wary in downtown kabul.
weighed down by combat boots,
wired to the sky,
dressed to kill.

kurd of the infamous video
uploaded from hell.
naked before the world.
your doomed blinking more terrible
than any blood.

pawns on what board,
knights on the hard road
to what holy city?

Majesty, where can love
hide its face?

pir's tomb deep in the cornfields

a motorcycle—quick!
i drop beside the recumbent saint, his instant wife,
until the danger's passed.

up and dust off my poloneck
bare-chested, change with it the balance of my life,
unshackled from the past.

leaving sikri

time to go,
and i think—take the *train!*
(the way lord curzon came)

now strictly for villagers.
even clerks
take the slightly dearer clapped out bus.

the bogey's packed to overflowing,
push come to shove.
but a crone makes room, clops

with her hand the wooden seat beside her,
turns a toothless smile on me,
her one good eye glowing.

the heart begins again to sing.
it's love all right, Majesty,
these assignations,

or the next best thing.

finis

Acknowledgements

Vivek Narayanan helped me sort wheat from tares.
Wayne Begley showed me a personal Akbar.
Irfan Habib schooled an amateur.
Ruby Lal twitched Akbar's harem curtain.
Surjit Das abandoned me in Fatehpur Sikri.
Anshu Vaish housed me in Lord Curzon's lodge.
Sharmistha Mohanty showed me Akbar's tomb.
Simar Puneet plied a fine-toothed comb.
Jalal-ud-din Akbar shone on me.
Dan O'Connor rallied me.
Irwin Sealy Sr taught me haunting.

Cushla tossed a small pierced coin.